# Seven Nights of Snuggles

Stories by Clare C-Saunders

Illustrated by Rose C-Saunders

ISBN: 1523951117
ISBN-13: 978-1523951116

# DEDICATION

To Rose and George, who inspired these stories…
I love you to the moon and stars, to the universe, to infinity
and beyond and back again.

# CONTENTS

# ACKNOWLEDGMENTS

Thank you to my wonderful children, Rose for her beautiful illustrations in this book, I hope you go on to do many more. George, for lighting up my life with your innocent questions, and our lovely Newfoundland puppy, Arthur Bear for his unlimited brown fur-baby cuddles, to all of you for being the inspiration behind this book. To my wonderful husband, Adam Saunders, thank you for putting up with me and my technical phobias and also for grammatically editing and formatting this book. Thank you to the team at CreateSpace. Thank you to my guardian angels for your help and guidance.

# 1

# THE ORANGE MONKEY

In a faraway land lived a pack of brown-coated monkeys. On a hot, sticky summer's day they all gathered together to celebrate the arrival of their newest baby monkeys. The first mummy monkey greeted her new baby boy with a joyful smile, delighted to see the little brown fluffy bundle in her arms. All the other brown furry monkeys looked on with pleasure at the newest additions to their all-brown pack. The second mummy monkey had a pretty little brown baby girl and cuddled her whilst filling up with glee. The rest of her pack cooed delightedly alongside her.

However, the third mummy monkey delivered an altogether different package. Her baby monkey was born bright orange! Mummy Monkey was puzzled, as everyone else in her pack was brown. But she loved her fuzzy orange baby all the same and with all her heart.

The rest of the pack did not feel the same way as Orange Monkey's mummy. They all gasped with horror at the latest arrival. "How disgusting! The nerve of him being born orange!" Behind Orange Monkey's back, the other monkeys said, "He will never fit in here. He just simply isn't one of us!"

As Orange Monkey grew up and went to school, he was made fun of by the other children for being different. He couldn't make any friends, as nobody wanted to also be laughed at by the rest of the pack. Poor, little Orange Monkey felt sad and alone. He tried to find ways of making his fur brown, like the other monkeys'. He rolled around in mud and dirt but ended up only with his beautiful orange fur clumping together tattily, giving the bullies even more to laugh about.

At the end of each school day, Orange Monkey greeted his mummy with a warm hug and cheery "hello." He would then lie to her, telling her he had a wonderful day at school. One day Mummy Monkey could tell something was wrong, but she knew nothing was stronger or more powerful than a mother's love and that she could help him through this. "Son, if you ever have a bad day at school, you know you can always tell me the truth, don't you?" Orange Monkey looked cautiously up at his mummy and tentatively began telling her the truth.

Mummy Monkey caringly reassured him, "Everything will

be all right. Just remember to always be true to yourself."
Orange Monkey wondered what she meant by this, but he felt better that he'd finally unburdened himself of lying. With no friends to play with, he decided he would entertain himself. He soon found out he could do extraordinary things the other monkeys could not do so well. After all, they were far too busy wasting their energy on making up unkind comments about Orange Monkey's differences and talking about how they were far superior to him. They had no time left to think or act creatively.

As little Orange Monkey grew into bigger Orange Monkey, eventually the time came to leave school. He breathed a welcome sigh of relief at the thought of never being forced into spending another moment with the bullies and their unwelcome comments about his ugly orangeness. He had worked very hard on all his monkey skills and lessons and was by far the cleverest monkey in his pack, not to mention the most talented and strong. Orange Monkey was strong on the inside as well as the outside because he had to put up with being different—and this made him determined to succeed.

Of course, having no friends might make one very lonely. One day Orange Monkey swung through the treetops to his safe place, where none of the other monkeys could reach him as they were afraid to climb so high. He sat on top of the highest tree and cried. Suddenly a beautiful big eagle flew up alongside him and asked, "Why on Earth is a monkey as special as you sitting up here alone, crying?" Orange Monkey explained all to Golden Eagle, who was a very wise and caring bird. Golden Eagle told Orange Monkey, "You have found a friend in me, and you no longer need to worry about being lonely. I know a place filled with animals like you."

"You mean there are other orange monkeys?"

"No, no, no…you misunderstand! I am not speaking of your colour or outer appearance, for that matters not here. What matters is that you are nice, kind, talented, and strong, but most of all you are exceptionally special! So why cry about the fact that you don't fit in on the ground— being boringly similar to everyone else is underrated, my friend—when it is perfectly clear to me that you should be flying with the eagles?"

Golden Eagle flew from branch to branch whilst Orange Monkey shone bright sparkling fiery-orange flashes, even brighter than the stars, as he swung alongside him. Orange Monkey had found his confidence—and a real friend. When they reached their final destination up in the hills, they were greeted by lots of other extraordinarily unique animals and birds.

Orange Monkey was very pleased to meet Purple Elephant, who could play the drums and trumpet his trunk at the same time.

He was delighted to meet Green Giraffe, who could roller-skate and sing.

Golden Eagle's bright gold wings fluttered with graceful shimmering magic through the skies.

Orange Monkey was quite the talented gymnast, and his orange fur flashed like a firework as he spun around to perform his tricks for his newfound friends.

The friends all decided it would be fun, with their special skills, to make up a show together. They made a giant rainbow-colour theatre on the ground, where all the other animals could come and watch.

They took turns showcasing their special gifts and talents to an appreciative audience. Orange Monkey felt nervous at first, especially when he peaked through the curtain and noticed his old pack sat in the crowd. With the help and support of his new friends, he went on to demonstrate there was a lot more to him than just being orange.

All the brown monkeys enjoyed Orange Monkey's performance so much that they couldn't help joining in and having fun. They clapped and cheered as Orange Monkey flew through the air and somersaulted in ways they couldn't have imagined possible and would never dare to attempt.

Afterwards, the all-brown pack congratulated Orange Monkey. "We never saw how amazing you are, because we couldn't see past what makes you different." They apologized to their orange friend and felt embarrassed for being mean to him in the past. All was forgiven between them and made right. The funny thing was that the brown monkeys now wanted to be like their fabulous friend, so they all found ingenious ways to look orange!

# 2

# BERTIE MOUSE AND WILY CAT

Once upon a time, there lived a sweet little mouse called Bertie. He lived in a modest little mouse hole with his mummy, daddy, and three sisters—Tilly, Flopsy, and Dora.

The six little mice all lived very happily together in their cosy little den. Mummy Mouse rocked and knitted in her favourite rocking chair, dressed in her lovely mop cap and matching pinny with lace trim and delicate embroidered flowers.

Daddy was very brave, and every day he ventured out of the mouse hole in search of food scraps left behind and forgotten by the human family who shared their home. Daddy Mouse had just one problem, and that was Wily Cat, the big fat grey feline with long pointy teeth. Wily was a cunning cat, who loved nothing more than to chase, catch, and eat mice!

Back in the mouse hole, Tilly, Flopsy, Dora, and Bertie enjoyed playing games together. They played tag, catch, marbles, hide-and-seek, and hopscotch, among many other fun activities involving their imaginations. The children loved to play dress-up in the fancy costumes they found around the house when it was safe to go out of the mouse hole, such as the times Wily Cat was taken to the vet.

It was a day such as this, when the mice thought they were safe, that this story takes place. As already mentioned, the hero of the story, Bertie, had a heart of gold. In fact he would have pulled the stars from the sky for his mummy if he could, but Bertie had one tiny little flaw. Bertie was not very good at listening and doing what he was told. Sometimes Bertie had stubborn tendencies and thought he knew best.

The problem was that little Bertie was growing overly confident in himself as the eldest brother to three silly sisters…or so he thought of them. Wily Cat became aware of this and decided to use it to his advantage.

Wily Cat bade his time, every day leaving a tasty scrap of cheese close to the little mouse hole. He placed the cheese a little farther from the mouse door each day so the mice would have to move farther and farther away from safety to get it. Wily Cat pretended to go out, but little did the unsuspecting mice know he was cunningly creeping back in through an open window and hiding. He kept a careful watch on the mice, patiently waiting for the day he could pounce on his unwitting prey.

Daddy Mouse became suspicious. "It seems a bit strange that Wily Cat is out so much nowadays, and every day that cheese appears to move farther away from our safety zone," he said to Mummy Mouse. "It's best the children stay in today while I try to figure this out."

Mummy Mouse told her beautiful children to stay safe inside the mouse hole until Daddy returned home. The children were bored being stuck inside. "Let's play dare!" suggested Bertie. The children giggled mischievously.

Flopsy dared Tilly to go try on Mummy's mop cap, which she did, and everybody laughed. Then Tilly dared Dora to hide Daddy's reading glasses, and they all giggled once again at their naughtiness. Next, Dora dared Bertie to stick his toe out of the mouse hole. Bertie decided to show off. "I'm the biggest here, and I'm far braver than that. I'm going to run and get that cheese Daddy brings back every day." *They'll all see how big and clever I am,* thought Bertie proudly.

Off he went, right into Wily Cat's cunning trap. As soon as poor, unknowing Bertie was far from the safety of his little mouse hole, Wily Cat made his move and pounced on him.

"Help!" cried Bertie to his three sisters as he hopelessly tried to fight off Wily Cat's long pointy teeth and smelly bad breath. Flopsy, Tilly, and Dora ran as fast as they could to their mummy and cried for help. Without a thought for her own safety, Mummy Mouse ran outside. Still holding her knitting needles, she poked Wily Cat straight in his bottom with the pointy ends. "Whoa! Ouch!" cried Wily Cat, who let go of Bertie to rub his bottom with his paws.

Daddy returned home just in time to grab little Bertie and run back into the hole alongside Mummy Mouse. "You were very lucky, Bertie, that your sisters were clever enough to do the right thing in telling Mummy you were in trouble. Next time you might not be so lucky if you don't listen to Mummy and Daddy and do what you are told. We love you and don't want you to get hurt. That's why we have rules. It's not to spoil your fun—it's to make sure you play safely."

Through sniffles and snivels, Bertie Mouse assured his family, "I'll never be so silly again. From now on, I'll do what I'm told." Mummy, Daddy, Tilly, Flopsy, and Dora gathered around Bertie and gave him a big, warm, fuzzy hug.

# 3

# GEORGE AND THE GIANT SUNFLOWER

This is George. He likes getting messy.

One sunny spring day, George's mummy gave him a very special sunflower seed. George enjoyed getting quite messy as he planted his sunflower seed in a little pot, using his spade and adding some soil and water.

"Did you enjoy getting messy?" asked George's mummy.

"Yes," George answered excitedly. "Will it grow higher and higher and higher and higher until it reaches the sky?"

With that special loving look in her eye, Mummy replied, "Maybe—you never know."

Every day George took great care of his sunflower. He watered it and gave it a lovely sunny place on his windowsill.

Then one day it began to grow...

and grow...

and grow...

…until it got too big for his window, and George had to plant it outside in his garden instead.

**"It's bigger than me!"**

In the daytime, the sun glittered beams of nourishing light onto George's much-loved sunflower. By night, with the light of the moon and her twinkling star companions, little drops of crystal rain tumbled down. George's sunflower loved the sun and rain, and it grew even more.

It grew higher…

and higher…

and higher…

…until it reached the sky!

"Do you see it, Mummy? It does reach the sky!"

George's mummy stood, open-mouthed, and looked at it.

"It's a giant!" declared George, and all his friends and neighbours had to agree!

# 4

# DOG AND BONE

At the end of the day Mummy would say,
"Put all of your things away.
Whosits in baskets and whatsits in drawers,
Pick everything up off the floors."
Daddy would nod in agreement but forget to do the same.

Daddy, being Cockney, would use rhyming slang.
"Up the apples and pears" meant go upstairs.
"Round little Jack Horner"—go round the corner.
"Treacle tart"—sweetheart!
Daddy hoped that someday I would learn it, too.

One day after Mummy had complained about the mess,
Me and my sister tidied up our very best.
Our home looked spotless—to us it looked amazing—
But still we saw our daddy red-faced and complaining!
"I lost my dog!" he moaned, befuddled and bemused.
"Here he is! I found him!"
"No, dear, you're confused! I meant my phone—the dog
and bone!"
So Mummy tried to ring it.

Daddy waited anxiously as Mummy began to dial.
Then something odd occurred that made me raise a smile.
"Daddy, Daddy, the dog is ringing!"
"Well done, son!" he said,
As he was delighted with my rhyming slang instead.
Then a look of horror hit him on his face,
turning into terror, proceeding to disgrace,

For doggy's tummy really rang—it rang and rang out loud.
He'd swallowed up his bone and was feeling rather proud.

# 5

## THE KINDNESS CAKE

Henry's family was very poor, scarcely affording food. His family members made up in acts of kindness, good deeds, and unselfishness for what they lacked in their pockets and piggy banks. One day Henry's mother asked him to take her last few coins and fetch some bread from the shop so she could make toast for supper. Henry took the last of the family's money and promised to be back soon.

As Henry walked down the lane, he noticed a chicken caught in some wire. Without hesitation he kindly freed the chicken's little foot. "Thank you," said the chicken. "I have been stuck for hours, and everyone else was in far too much of a hurry to notice me or stop to help if they did. For your act of kindness, please accept my lovely eggs as a thank-you gift." Henry gratefully accepted, thanking the chicken, and then continued on his way.

Next, Henry noticed a little old lady struggling with heavy bags and trying to put her key in the door. Henry offered to unlock the door for her. "Oh, thank you," said the little old lady. "I have been fumbling about for hours with this little old key. I forgot my glasses today and could not find the lock. My heavy bags of flour made it all the more difficult, as I could not place them on the ground for fear of getting them wet. Please take a couple of bags of flour for yourself as a thank-you for your kindness." Henry gratefully accepted and bid the lady farewell.

When Henry eventually arrived at the shop, he noticed the shopkeeper was very busy picking up spilt stock and putting it back on shelves. Henry helped the man, who was struggling to reach from the ladder with heavy bags of sugar in his hands. "Thank you for being so kind. I'm afraid we had a little old lady in here earlier who couldn't seem to see where she was going and knocked all my sugar bags over whilst reaching for flour. It would have taken me all day to clean this mess up without your help. I tell you what—please take a couple of bags of sugar as a thank-you for your kindness." Henry gratefully accepted and then handed the shopkeeper the last of his family's money for bread.

Henry happily hurried home to his mother. He presented her with his goodies, whilst regaling her with stories of his travels. His mother was delighted with her little boy. "Henry, not only do we have bread, but with all your ingredients, now I can even bake a cake from all your acts of kindness! We'll call it the 'kindness cake,' and I'd like you to deliver a piece to all those you helped as a thank-you for their contribution."

So his mother baked a beautiful cake, and Henry went out to find the little chicken. He gave her a piece, explaining what had happened. The chicken was delighted and, in return, gave Henry even more eggs!

Henry visited the little old lady, delivering to her a piece of the cake. She made him a cup of tea, whilst he told her all about how he'd got the ingredients by helping those in need and that he'd never expected anything in return. The little old lady gave Henry two more bags of flour and asked that he visit again next time his mother made cake, as she enjoyed his company.

Next, Henry delivered some cake to the shopkeeper. He told him about his adventures helping people who in return had given him little gifts. Henry went on to explain that the little gifts added up to create a huge kindness cake for everyone.

The shopkeeper loved the idea of Henry's kindness cake, and he offered to buy more cake from Henry and his mother to sell in his shop. Henry's mother was delighted, and the cake was so yummy that all the villagers went to the shop to buy some. Henry was offered a job in the shop to help sell the cake, and his family was never poor again.

All because of a few small acts of kindness, improving the world a little bit at a time, Henry's kind gestures soon mounted up to make a big difference!

# 6

# JACK'S GIGANTIOUS CATERPILLAR

Jack loved to play outside. He loved climbing trees and playing in muddy water with his wellies on, and he especially enjoyed looking for bugs to frighten his mummy with!

Yes, little Jack was a bit mischievous that way, but he was a kind and generous boy, and everyone loved him very much.

One day while Jack played in his garden, he came across a fuzzy green caterpillar. He did not know what it was, so he thought he would keep an eye on his new little friend. He picked up the caterpillar and placed it in a special little bug garden he had made out of rocks and grass. Jack found a cabbage leaf in the kitchen and offered it to his new friend. The caterpillar ate it up and seemed to really enjoy it.

The next day Jack went outside, with another cabbage leaf, to his special bug garden. The caterpillar gobbled it up straight away and, looking for more, turned to Jack. Jack didn't want his friend to go hungry, so he went back to the fridge, but all the cabbage was gone!

Suddenly Jack remembered his daddy had a special supply of cabbages in the greenhouse, but Jack wasn't supposed to eat it under any circumstances. *Well, it can't hurt if I feed it to my caterpillar, as, technically, I won't be the person eating it,* Jack thought. He decided his plan was very clever, as he sneakily stole a couple of large juicy leaves. "Cor! These cabbages are so big they are like giants, they are gigantious! Here you go my little friend this should fill you up."

Jack fed the leaves to his friendly caterpillar, which greedily gobbled them up.

The next morning, Jack went outside again to check on his friend. The caterpillar seemed to have doubled in size overnight. "Wow! You were having a growth spurt—that's why you were so hungry. My mummy always says that if you eat your greens, you will grow up big and strong. She's right, too—just look at you!"

Jack took his caterpillar with him to choose some more of Daddy's cabbage leaves. He very carefully picked up his friend and cuddled it under his arms, rather like a small dog.

The cabbages in the greenhouse also seemed to have doubled in size overnight and were twice as large as any Jack had seen before in his fridge or at the local Greengrocers shop. "There you are—help yourself!" Jack told his cuddly, fuzzy green caterpillar, gently laying it down next to the grotesquely oversize cabbages. At that, the caterpillar greedily devoured a whole, entire cabbage! "Oh, my goodness!" cried Jack. "You weren't supposed to eat the whole thing. I hope Daddy doesn't notice there's one missing." Jack lovingly reprimanded his friend and arranged the remaining cabbages to close the gap where the now-eaten cabbage had been.

Jack showed his friendly caterpillar all around his favourite places. They enjoyed climbing trees and playing in muddy puddles until the sun started to set. Placing his friend back into its snuggly bug bed, he tucked it in with grass and leaves. Jack said, "Good night," and went to his own bed to sleep.

In the morning, Jack hurried out of bed as fast as he could and gobbled down his breakfast. He couldn't wait to see his friend again. However, when Jack arrived at the bug bed, the caterpillar was no longer there!

Jack could find only a huge, ugly-looking object. It was longer than two large snakes and fatter than three fat pigs, and there was no head nor tail! It certainly was not cute, green, and fuzzy either. Oh no—this thing was grey and hairy and didn't look very nice at all! *Oh, my goodness! I…I killed my best friend!* Jack's thoughts were jumbled and running wild. Confused, he ran to his daddy as fast as his feet would take him, tears streaming down his face.

Jack found his daddy at work in the greenhouse. The cabbages had grown so big and fat now that his daddy had to move the leaves away from his eyes and struggle through them to find Jack and cuddle him. Caringly, Daddy asked, "Whatever is the matter, Jack?"

Jack explained the whole thing. "And so you see, Daddy, it was all my fault. If I hadn't been a naughty boy and fed your prize-winning, gigantious cabbages to my best friend, I wouldn't have killed him. I'm so sorry." Jack sobbed. Daddy turned pale and looked, horrified, at the nearly empty bottle of liquid he had been using to make his cabbages grow as large, fast, and perfect as they could— much larger and faster than nature would allow. In Daddy's eyes, the cabbages were much prettier than a naturally grown vegetable without perfect leaves like those on his cabbages. If only he had thought about the ill effects of spraying chemicals onto food!

"Oh, dear son, I am so sorry, too. If I hadn't used this silly spray all over these cabbages then your lovely friend would surely still be alive." Jack sadly took his daddy by the hand and led him to the bug bed. Daddy looked up, terrified, and could not believe his eyes! "Son, what did your friend look like before?"

Through his sobs, Jack tried to answer. "Well, he was lovely…and fuzzy…and green."

Realization washed over Daddy's face, and relief settled in his stomach, as it became apparent that his prize-winning experimental growth and vegetable-perfecting formula hadn't killed the little boy next door as he'd thought. "Son, I don't believe your friend is dead at all." Surprised, Jack looked up at his Daddy, who said, "I believe your fuzzy, green, cabbage-loving friend was a caterpillar, Jack. This is his giant chrysalis! Let's leave your friend in peace and return later on."

A couple weeks passed, and Jack felt sad. He missed his best friend and still wasn't entirely convinced he hadn't hurt it. *Maybe Daddy made up all that chrysalis nonsense to make me feel better.*

Kicking up leaves, Jack shuffled sadly along the pathway to the bug bed. He heard a noise and stopped suddenly. The horrid, grey, crusty thing began to crack. Jack stood, terrified. His feet felt glued to the ground, like in a nightmare when he couldn't run away. This time, however, it was real. Unable to move through his fear, knees trembling, Jack didn't want to look up at it but couldn't help himself. He couldn't peel his eyes off as it cracked some more. Gungy liquid spewed out of it, followed by a very long, grey, hairy leg and then another. Another two shorter legs emerged, followed by a very scary-looking couple of antennae. Jack stood frozen as two beady eyes peeked at him and the crusty shell cracked all the way open. Jack wanted to scream, but he couldn't.

Suddenly a familiar fuzzy, green face stared upside down at him. "Hello!" his friend remarked. "Oh, I had the best sleep ever!" A bit of slime drizzled down its furry cheek and plopped on Jack's nose. Then the most beautiful, amazing thing happened. Jack felt his jaw drop as his friend unfurled the most magnificent rainbow-colour wings. Emerging from this disgusting-looking shell was the most spectacular butterfly Jack had ever seen! "You are gigantious!" Jack exclaimed, "Just like Daddy's cabbages that you ate!"

Jack's best friend was back, bigger and better than ever. His mesmerizing rainbow wings were as big as Daddy's greenhouse. The butterfly took Jack under its wing, gently cuddling him, and they took off and flew around all of Jack's favourite places. They landed from time to time on the tallest tree branches, which Jack had always tried to climb but never quite had the courage to reach until now…with the help of his best friend, who everyone came to know as Jack's gigantious caterpillar.

# 7

# THE PRINCESS FAIRY'S
# SPECTACULAR SPECTACLES

In a magical land far, far away from our own, lived a beautiful princess fairy. Her name was Rose, because that was the flower she grew inside of before she was born to the king and queen of the Gnome Kingdom.

Rose was a very popular little girl within all the kingdom. However, she was very clumsy and had the unfortunate ability to cause a lot of accidents. One day when she was practicing for her fairy-wings flying (grade one) exam, she bumped into the palace baker and knocked over all the fairy cakes for the royal ball.

Another time, whilst learning how to use her magic star wand, she accidentally turned the palace cat into a roaring tiger with purple wings. Imagine how many people it took to capture it so her teacher could correct the mistake!

Another time she mistook the fairy flying dust for sneezing powder. This left her family sneezing for hours until it wore off.

"Something has to be done about our lovely Rose," the king declared to his queen.

"Yes, but what?" the queen asked, baffled.

The palace optician overheard this discussion. "Perhaps, sire, I may be able to help. Might I suggest she try these spectacular spectacles?"

Rose tried on her new pink glasses, which sparkled and glittered in the fairy lights of the palace. Everyone in the kingdom agreed they looked splendid. Best of all, though, they worked!

Rose could now see where she was going! When she was flying, she no longer knocked over all the fairy cakes and the palace baker. Rose practiced and practiced her fairy-wings flying, grade one, and passed her exam with *flying colours*!

Now that her focus was better, Rose could aim her star wand magnificently on target, leaving the palace cat and all the servants very peaceful and happy.

Finally she could read the labels on the potion bottles, and she never again mixed up the fairy dust and the sneezing powder. The king and queen were very relieved, and everyone—especially Rose!—was delighted with the princess fairy's spectacular spectacles.

# ABOUT THE AUTHOR

Clare C-Saunders discovered her love of writing children's stories whilst running her own successful children's entertainment business. Clare wrote original pantomime-style shows and performed them for children at special events. Through the storytelling in her shows and also taking inspiration from her children and their friends, Clare came up with the concept of *Seven Nights of Snuggles*. The idea behind the book is that all busy parents can spend a few precious moments with their children as part of the bedtime routine, cuddling up with a short story. The book is also designed to be small so it can be carried with the reader on holiday. The familiarity is then reassuring whilst away from home and can help children settle down at bedtime.

Clare has strong beliefs that children should have a childhood filled with joy and outdoor fun instead of being force-fed exams and sitting inside all day to stare at a computer screen. These stories are also inspired by Clare's experience as a parent of children who attended a Steiner Waldorf kindergarten, which shares this philosophy.

# ABOUT THE STORIES

Each story has its own little message to tell your children:

**"The Orange Monkey"** reassures each child that it is OK to be yourself and enjoy your own uniqueness. It's what makes everyone special.

**"Bertie Mouse and Wily Cat"** is a lesson on safety and following parents' guidance.

**"George and the Giant Sunflower"** was inspired by Clare's son, George, who asked if his sunflower seed would grow higher and higher and higher until it reached the sky. It also carries the message of outdoor fun, inspiring creativity and imagination.

**"Dog and Bone"** was borne out of Clare's family's Newfoundland puppy eating her husband's new phone and is a lesson to all parents not to leave things out but to tidy away like the children do!
**"The Kindness Cake"** demonstrates how small acts of kindness add up and how good karma works.

**"Jack's Gigantious Caterpillar"** has a message about hidden chemicals in our food and their unknown effects. This story is pro organic and pro "ugly" fruit and vegetables, as nature intended. It is also a tale of empathy and caring for a pet while having outdoor adventures. In a nod to Clare's favourite children's author, Roald Dahl, the author decided to make up a word and add a bit of scariness to this story!

**"The Princess Fairy's Spectacular Spectacles"** was written for Clare's daughter, Rose, when she was prescribed glasses for the first time. Rose was watching a well-known children's film in which a princess has her glasses removed during a makeover. Rose asked, "Mummy, why are they taking her glasses off her?" As a mummy, Clare felt her heart sink at this shallow message of beauty and vanity over intelligence being put out to young girls everywhere. She decided to write the opposite, giving girls a heroine whose glasses improve her abilities and intelligence.

25136732R00026

Printed in Great Britain
by Amazon